READING WITH PURPOSE

ABOUT THE AUTHOR

NANCY WILSON IS A PASTOR'S WIFE AND FORMER LITERATURE TEACHER AT LOGOS SCHOOL IN MOSCOW, IDAHO. HER THREE CHILDREN GRADUATED FROM LOGOS SCHOOL AND SHE CURRENTLY HAS NUMEROUS GRANDCHILDREN WHO ATTEND THERE AS WELL.

————————————————

Published by Logos Press
207 N Main St, Moscow, Idaho 83843
www.logospressonline.com

Nancy Wilson, *Reading with a Purpose: Applying the Christian Worldview to American Literature*
Copyright ©2003, 2021 by Nancy Wilson

Cover and interior design by Megan Mason

Printed in the United States of America.

21 22 23   4 3 2

READING WITH PURPOSE

APPLYING THE CHRISTIAN WORLDVIEW TO AMERICAN LITERATURE

NANCY WILSON

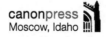
canonpress
Moscow, Idaho

CONTENTS

PREFACE

When I was studying English literature as an undergraduate, I had a spiritual crisis. My professors were teaching a view of man that I could not refute. One professor in particular repeatedly taught us that man was just a beast, beyond hope, with no purpose in life but to reproduce. He accepted this view with a cool despair, but I became more and more troubled. What was my purpose? Did life have any ultimate meaning? If so, how could I find out what it was?

Literature always expresses a view about God, man, nature, and the world because it deals with ultimate questions. Ungodly instructors and writers can press unbelieving ideas upon students and readers with great force and persuasiveness, especially when the class is not grounded on a solid foundation. Students who are not *thinking Christians* can be lead to believe many untrue things. Christians who study or teach or just read literature must learn to *think like Christians* and apply it to all they read. Because I did not know what was true about God, about man, and about the universe, I was tossed about and troubled and misled. But, thanks be to God, He used the ungodly view of man to lead me to Himself and set me on a firm foundation.

Because I have seen the destructive nature of literature when not studied from a Christian worldview, it was a great delight to me, years later, to be a high-school literature instructor myself. My goal has been to equip students to love literature while loving Christ more. When we understand how to examine the worldview of the writer and consider it from a Christian perspective, we are then free to stay uncontaminated by ungodly thinking while appreciating all that is good in the work.

It is my hope that this little booklet will be of special help to Christian teachers and parents

who want their students to enjoy literature as one
of God's many gifts to us, while thinking about all
they read *Christianly*.

~ Nancy Wilson

WHY READ ANYWAYS?

Before we can discuss *how* to read Christianly, we must consider a more fundamental question: Why should we read at all? What is the purpose of literacy? Most parents are eager to see their children reading as early as possible, but why? Is it to keep their children busy so they can entertain themselves? What is the goal of literacy?

The non-Christian has only two options here. He can read for pleasure and entertainment, which is hedonism, or he can read for reading's sake, which is aestheticism. Reading for pleasure is just like anything else that is done strictly for the enjoyment of the creature: it turns into worship of the creature. Hedonism is the view that I exist to please myself. Therefore, if reading pleases me, then I will read. Reading is seen as the means to an end: pleasure.

Aestheticism is the worship of art for art's sake. This is obviously another dead end. This view sees reading not as a means to an end, but an end in itself. Bookishness can be seen as worldly sophistication: to speak of books and authors and poetry over coffee, to hold a fine volume in the hand, to display an impressive library, the result of years of ardent collecting. When this is not done to the glory of God, it is obviously idolatry. A huge mahogany library stashed from floor to ceiling with leather-bound books is appealing to us all; but that shouldn't be enough for the Christian. Without a right understanding of God and a deep gratitude to Him for His gifts, this is just one more hollow attempt to find meaning in a seemingly meaningless world.

Though Christians can certainly be entertained by reading, find great pleasure in reading, and love the beauty of expression in a work, they have a much more profound reason to appreciate literature than the unbeliever: the glory and pleasure of God. When a Christian is deliberately trying to take every thought captive for Christ, books can be a source of great pleasure and joy without being a form of idolatry. Believers have the opportunity to enjoy life, including literature, in a way the unbeliever cannot. God enables the Christian to feast gratefully on the many blessings He bestows while giving the glory back to Him. This means that if we think carefully about books, and think rightly about God, literature can be richly enjoyed like all God's other gifts.

Christians, of all people, should *love* books. God Himself is the Creator of words, His Son is the Word, and we have God's precious Word to us in the Scriptures. Words for Christians have special significance because they are part of God's revelation to us. And He has created us to love stories and storytelling as part of our creature-hood. This love of stories can be used and delighted in to His glory and praise. After all, the Bible is a collection of stories. The Gospel is Christ's story. It is *The Story*. And Jesus Himself is the Master Storyteller.

WHAT IS THE CHRISTIAN VIEW OF LITERATURE?

Christians have been discussing and defending a right use of literature for centuries. Some have argued that fiction is an ungodly form of writing because it is not true, because it is morally corrupting, or because it is purely recreational and therefore useless. Sir Philip Sidney ably defended the use of fiction in his treatise *A Defense of Poesy* written in the 1580's. As he points out, Christ used parables to teach during His earthly ministry. Fiction, he says, does not purport to be true, like history does, and is better suited to teach and delight than any other form of writing. C.S. Lewis, in *The Discarded Image*, echoes Sidney when he says, "Literature exists to teach what is useful, to honour what deserves honour, to appreciate the delightful. The useful, honourable, and delightful are superior to it: it exists for their sake; its own use, honour, or delightfulness is derivative from theirs."

Unbelievers have written much about literature, but it is important for Christians who are studying literature to develop a Christian view about the purpose of literature. Examining what writers like Sidney and Lewis have said is a valuable way to begin thinking about this. Consider the quote from Lewis above. Like Sidney, he believed literature should teach something useful. Some may think this is obvious, but many authors have felt strongly to the contrary. For example, Edgar Allan Poe believed literature should not be didactic, but should rather attempt to have one impact or effect. In Poe's case, he wanted to scare the reader to death. The American imagists (1901-1918) agreed with Poe that literature should not teach. They believed a poem should exist the same way a piece of fruit exists: it simply is. Archibald MacLeish, writing in 1892 in his poem "Ars Poetica," says, "A poem should not mean But be."

Both these views are impossible, for teaching something is inescapable. When you say poetry should not teach, you are, after all, teaching what poetry should be. Literature cannot be an end in itself; it must either glorify God or it will glorify something else.

According to Lewis's definition of literature, it exists for the sake of something other than itself: the useful, the honourable, and the delightful. In other words, literature reflects the glory of these things; it does not have any glory of its own. And the useful, honourable, and delightful glorify God. When we elevate literature above these things, we end up with the literary equivalent of modern art: words splattered across the page that distort truth, goodness, and beauty. For the Christian, literature is a means of knowing more about God and His world and should result in more glory for Him. In the Christian's pursuit of truth, goodness, and beauty, literature should have a key role. Is the story or poem saying true things about God, man, and the world? That would make it useful. Is it embracing the good? That would make it honorable. And is it beautiful? That would make it delightful. This is what Christians should look for in literature. Without these things, literature fails to glorify God, for He cannot be pleased with falsehood, badness, and ugliness. Nor should we be.

So why should Christians read non-Christian writers? Of course we should be discriminating readers. But we cannot understand our world if we refuse to engage with the history of ideas. And even non-Christians have things to teach us. They can help us to understand the world through their eyes, enabling us to see the consequences of sin, the extent of spiritual blindness, and the need for the gospel. But God has shed His grace abroad, and even unbelievers can have extraordinary gifts in literature. Thus we can appreciate the common grace exhibited in the world. We can "plunder the Egyptians" and freely take the treasures offered in their writing. How else can we identify false ideas and teach our students to refute them if they never come into contact with any? The Apostle Paul was familiar with the classical literature of his day, and he quotes from three poets in Acts 17 (Epimenides, Cleanthes, and Aratus). If we are to be missionaries to our culture, we must understand it. The sermons and writings of the Puritans are saturated with references from classical literature. They understood this principle of being enriched in their understanding of God's world by being unafraid to study literature, even that written by unbelievers. For example, the Puritan Matthew Henry quotes from Ovid's *Art of Love* in his book called *The Quest For Meekness and Quietness of Spirit*. If this book were in the high-school reading list, it would make parents jumpy, and for good reason! The Puritans truly understood how to read and make use of pagan literature. It is inevitable that we will have imagination, but we Christians should strive for sanctified imaginations: those that are trained not corrupted.

R.L. Dabney, the nineteenth-century theologian, wrote the essay entitled "On Dangerous Reading" where he warns Christians of the hazards of reading without thinking Christianly. His day was particularly ridden with sentimental, sappy novels that were not just a waste of time, but morally corrupting. As he points out, "So it is perfectly easy to paint truth at the bottom and error at the top when falsehood holds the brush." Here he is attacking the popularity of evil characters that were portrayed as heroes, arousing the sympathy of the casual reader. This is no different today. Christian people can find themselves sympathizing with evil characters in films and books if they do not pay attention. As a pastor, Dabney was gravely concerned for the spiritual health of his people. It is worthwhile to read his treatment of this subject. Christians have been struggling to have a right view and right use of literature for centuries. We should join into this discussion by reading all we can that Christians have already written about the subject. (A bibliography in the back of this booklet lists a few books you might find helpful.)

WHAT IS THE CHRISTIAN WORLDVIEW?

A worldview is, quite simply, the way one views the world. It is the paradigm a person has, whether consciously or unconsciously, by which he interprets all of his experience. In literature we can categorize the author's worldview as the view of God, man, and the world (or nature) that is expressed in the work. (We could also include many sub-categories, such as the view of sin, the atonement, and revelation.) A Christian worldview is that view of the world that is taught and laid out in the Bible. To oversimplify for this discussion, a Christian views God as the Creator and Sustainer of the universe, man as a fallen and sinful being who can be reconciled to God through Christ, and nature as a created thing that reflects God's glory. In other words, the Christian does not view God as an impersonal force, or fate; nor does he view Him as a benevolent and benign Creator who made the world but does not sustain it by His own power.

Unfortunately, many Christians do not know what the Bible teaches. It is impossible for them to have a Christian worldview, for they do not know much about God or about His dealings with man and the world. These readers assume that if a work mentions God, then it must be written by a Christian. This is a tremendous handicap, for it makes them prey to many of the world's false ideas, whether evolution or egalitarianism or the social gospel.

When I am teaching literature, whether a poem, essay, short story, or book, I instruct my students to be continually asking two questions: What is the author saying (about God, man, and nature)? Is it true? This is a good habit of mind to cultivate no matter what the student is reading—even if it's the back of the cereal box, something is being said. What is it? Is it true? This discipline should be carried over to film-watching as well. Thinking like Christians as we read is morally beneficial. It teaches us to apply our faith to everything.

Of course it is not only possible, but also sadly common in our day for Christians to write ungodly stories, poems, etc. The ungodliness can come in the form of sappy sentimentalism; it can be just crummy writing; or it can put forth ungodly views of Scripture and of God Himself. Christians need to be motivated and instructed to write beautiful, good, and true stories, not cheesy novels where everyone gets "saved" in the end. The Christian faith is much too glorious to be reduced to such unworthy levels. A good case in point is the popular *Left Behind* Series.

These books have sold millions of copies around the world, and this series lauded as great Christian literature. This is appalling. Not only do these books espouse unbiblical views of the end times, but they are also sappy, sentimental, and very poorly written.

Obviously, not every work will address every

question. A short poem about a leaf may not say much at all about these ultimate questions. On the other hand, it may reveal much of the author's worldview. Longer works cannot keep from exposing the author's worldview.

Sometimes several works must be read before the author's worldview can be understood. Some works may reveal much about the author's view of the nature of man, but say little directly about his view of God. But if you believe that man is basically good, then many things you believe about God will necessarily follow. If man is not in need of a savior (which is what those who think man is good must say), then Christianity has little to offer. I am not suggesting that we pull things out of context or try to read into works what is not there. Rather, I am saying we must look for the obvious things and train our minds to be always examining whether the true, the good, and the beautiful are evident.

LITERARY MOVEMENTS IN HISTORY

When I have discussed these ideas with teachers, I have often been asked if there is any simple, short booklet that summarizes different common worldviews in literature. Not knowing of any, I am attempting here to lay out some of the basic ideas of the larger historical literary periods in American literature to help teachers and students develop an overview. I will use American literature simply because I am most familiar with it, and once these concepts are understood, they apply to any literature. This does not mean that I do not think classical literature is important in the study of worldview; its worldview is crude polytheism, a despairing skepticism, and philosophical monotheism (no personal god). Nor do I lightly pass over British literature prior to America's founding. Much of it is deeply Christian. The writing of the Middle Ages is largely Christian, and the Renaissance has a dominant Christian worldview. But I am merely using American literature as a model to help train teachers to see how to recognize the worldviews in all kinds of literature.

This will necessarily have to be an oversimplification, but, Lord willing, it will enable both teacher and student to place books and authors in context. Dates used for the periods are based on those from the *Oxford Companion to American Literature*, as well as *The Harper Handbook to Literature*. An important book to read to understand American thinking is *A Theological Interpretation of American History* by C. Gregg Singer. This is a detailed and scholarly explanation of the patterns of thought from our founding to the present. (The Bob Jones literature textbooks, though I do not recommend them unreservedly, might be helpful to you in this regard.)

Each period of literature, even if it is predominantly non-Christian, will have Christian writers who do not espouse the prevailing views. Just as we live in Postmodern times and are affected by the thinking of our day, we strive to think like Christians in an unbelieving age. Thus, some authors in a period will be more openly ungodly than others. This much is obvious.

Each of these periods has been identified by historians as they have looked back and observed general trends, social and religious climates, and styles of writing. Within some of the larger movements are smaller sub-groups. Thus, this overview is not intended to be exhaustive. (At the end of each section I have included a small handful of other authors or works to help you get started.) As I have told my students, studying literature cannot be done apart from studying history and philosophy. It is important that the serious student of literature come to understand many philosophical terms as well as literary terms. It is impossible to examine a worldview without teaching your students the philosophical and historical context of each of these periods; this equips them to understand the mindset of the authors whose works they are reading. At the same time, realize that these are general characteristics and may not apply to each particular reading.

TIMELINE FOR AMERICAN LITERATURE

Colonial or Early American literature: 1607-1750

Neoclassicism: 1750-1820

American Romanticism: 1820-1865

American Realism and Naturalism: 1865-1920

Modern Period: 1914-1965

Postmodern: 1965-Present

EARLY AMERICAN LITERATURE

Seventeenth-century American writing is distinguished by its God-centeredness. It assumes a Protestant worldview in its various British forms: Anglican, Puritan, and nonconformist. All three were Calvinistic in theology; their differences lay largely in their views of church government. It is important for students to understand these differences, but it is not my purpose here to discuss them. Seventeenth-century British Americans assumed a divine Providence who graciously governed all of His creation. They had a pervasive view of Providence (God's sovereign control over His creation).

Though an in-depth understanding is not required, it is helpful for students to be generally familiar with the points of Calvinism to understand the early writings of this period. These can be summarized as follows:

1. *Total inability*: Man is completely unable to save himself.

2. *Sovereign election*: God sovereignly elects some to salvation, not based on man's works.

3. *Particular redemption*: Christ died to se cure the salvation of His elect.

4. *Resurrecting grace*: His grace is effectual in bringing the dead to life.

5. *Preservation of the saints*: Those whom God calls, He preserves to the end.

These have been called the doctrines of grace. Many of our founding fathers, even if they were not personally regenerate, assumed the claims of Calvinism to be true. Many who were persecuted for their faith in England and elsewhere came to America to worship freely, and they wrote about God's providential care for them in all things. Writers in this period of American literature viewed the Scriptures as the ultimate authority; they viewed man as a sinner in need of redemption; and they viewed nature as part of God's creation. They considered their purpose to glorify and honor God in all things.

Such American writers include William Bradford (a nonconformist), John Winthrop (a Puritan), Puritan poets Anne Bradstreet and Edward Taylor, Samuel Sewall, Mary Rowlandson, and others. Even Captain John Smith writes with reference to Providence. Consider the examples below.

William Bradford, in his historical account *Of Plymouth Plantation*, records the settlement of Plymouth from a religious point of view. The Puritans (a term which can include the nonconformists or pilgrims) saw all that transpired as from the hand of God, so when writing about this small colony, Bradford does not try to separate the events from the faith of the men and women involved.

Here are three samples from chapter eleven. Speaking of Squanto, Bradford says, "[he] was a special instrument sent of God for their good beyond their expectation." Later in the same chapter he records, "...it pleased God the mortality began to cease amongst them..." And again, "But it was the Lord which upheld them, and had beforehand prepared them; many having long borne the yoke, yea from their youth." A modern history text would not be filled with references to the Almighty's hand, though He is still at work in the world. Today, because of our faith in science, we want facts and data with no reference to God. This would have been foreign indeed to 17th century America.

In his brilliant essay on liberty, John Winthrop, deputy governor of Massachusetts Bay Colony, explains how all authority is from God and under God. He uses the picture of biblical marriage and the relationship the church has to Christ to illustrate his point. If you read the correspondence between Winthrop and his wife Margaret, it is clear they viewed their move to the New World as an attempt to establish an English Christian colony. Their letters are characterized by a humble, obedient love of Christ. (Some of these letters can be found in James Anderson's *Memorable Women of the Puritan Times*, vol. 1.)

The first book to be printed in Cambridge was the Psalter in 1640. As soon as the necessities of life were provided, the Puritans set about establishing Harvard College in 1636 to ensure that men called to the ministry would be educated, "dreading to leave an illiterate ministry to the churches when our present ministers shall lie in the dust." (This is from *New England's First Fruits*, included in *The American Puritans, Their Prose and Poetry*, edited by Perry Miller.)

The second rule laid down at Harvard was the following: "Let every student be plainly instructed and earnestly pressed to consider well: the main end of his life and studies is 'to know God and Jesus Christ, which is eternal life' (John 17.3), and therefore to lay Christ in the bottom, as the only foundation of all sound knowledge and learning. And seeing the Lord only giveth wisdom, let everyone seriously set himself by prayer in secret to seek it of Him

(Prov. 2.3)." Imagine one of our modern universities adopting such a rule today.

Both Anne Bradstreet and Edward Taylor were early colonial poets who expressed their faith through their poetry. Taylor, a pastor in Massachusetts, wrote meditations to prepare to serve the Lord's Supper. In these he expresses his love, devotion, and utter dependence on God, as well as his own unworthiness of God's blessing. Bradstreet contemplates the Lord's dealings in her life and in the lives of her children. (To read more about Bradstreet, see *Beyond Stateliest Marble*, by Douglas Wilson.)

Samuel Sewall, who served as Chief Justice of Massachusetts from 1718-1728, repented of his participation in the Salem witchcraft trials. This is an excerpt from the bill he wrote which was read publicly: "He...desires to take the blame and shame of it, asking pardon of men; and especially desiring prayers that God, who has an Unlimited Authority, would pardon that sin and all other his sins, personal and relative; and according to His infinite Benignity, and Sovereignty, not visit the sin of him, or of any other, upon himself or any of his, nor upon the land..." Imagine our leaders today repenting in such a manner. What a blessing it would be!

When Mary Rowlandson records her captivity and release from the Indians (published as *The Sovereignty and Goodness of God*), she cites many Scriptures that comforted her, and she comments on the Lord's provision for her throughout her trial. "But God was with me, in a wonderfull manner, carrying me along, and bearing up my spirit, that it did not quite fail."

Even the notorious John Smith acknowledges God's control of events. "But almighty God (by his divine providence) had mollified the hearts of those stern barbarians with compassion." (From *A General History*, chapter 2.)

Though Puritan writings may be difficult, they are very rewarding for the Christian because they record much that can inspire and instruct us as we view their faith from this distance. A book that can provide a rich background for students reading the Puritans is *The Worldly Saints* by Leland Ryken. Christian students find they have much in common with the Puritans, and this provides a valuable foundation for going on to read other books (like *The Scarlet Letter*) that portray the Puritans in an unflattering manner. Ryken considers both the strengths and weaknesses of the Puritans, so students are helped in their analysis of Puritan writing.

Reading works from this period is fairly simple when it comes to analyzing worldview because these are blatantly Christian. But even when the authors are Christian, it is wise to be reading carefully and critically. Some Puritans tended to become morbidly introspective.

This is good to bear in mind when reading authors like Michael Wigglesworth who understood man's depravity and God's judgment quite well, but emphasized God's grace and forgiveness too little. Again, Ryken's book is helpful is assessing the negative aspects of the Puritans.[1]

---

1. A few other suggested readings from this period (besides those listed above) include the following: John Smith authored *A True Relation*, *A Description of New England*, and *General Historie*. Though you may not want the students to read the entire works, you can certainly include excerpts from these. You can still obtain copies of the collected works of Anne Bradstreet and Edward Taylor.

NEOCLASSICISM

The general dates for Neoclassicism in England are 1660-1798, but America followed behind England, so the dates given for American literature are significantly later (1750-1820). Americans were busy establishing a country, achieving first religious freedom and then political independence. Even so, as we move from one period to another, we must realize it was a gradual transition spanning many years. It is not as though Neoclassicism arrived overnight. As men gradually compromise their beliefs, the consequences usually take a generation or two to manifest themselves. The Puritans failed to preserve the integrity and purity of the church. We can learn from their compromises as we try today to regain much lost territory in our country's faith.

Much can be said (and has been written) about this interesting and productive movement in literature. Called the Age of Reason or the Enlightenment, this period elevated human intellect above divine revelation as the source of all knowledge. This authority shift from God's Word to man's reason (rationalism or Deism) is entirely antithetical to biblical theology.

Deism allows for a Creator, but denies the Puritan idea of Providence. God is seen as benevolent Creator who made the world but rules it indirectly through the natural laws He established. He is described as the great clock-winder, fashioning the world and then setting it to run of its own accord. Jesus is viewed as a good man, a great moral teacher, but not the Incarnate Son of God.

Deism holds that man can know all that can be known by observing these natural laws in the world and using his own reason to understand them. In other words, God does not communicate to man through His Word, but man can use his own reason (enlightened by nature around him) to understand God. Miracles must also have a rational, logical explanation. The Bible is viewed as a good moral guide, but not considered to be accurate historically, nor inspired by God.

Deism asserts that man is basically good, not fallen, and, thus, though he is not perfect, he is perfectible through moral teaching. This emphasis on man's goodness is seen in Benjamin Franklin's writing; he used his *Poor Richard's Almanac* and *The Way to Wealth* to teach his fellow citizens to be good. The way to eradicate evil was seen to be through education, so much writing of this period was didactic, devoted to teaching man to be a better citizen. In other words, man's reason alone will lead him to virtuous conduct, so if we appeal to his reason, we can get him to change. We still are dealing with the consequences of this false idea in our day. Just telling man how to be good does not change his heart. Franklin himself saw the failure of his plan for his own perfection (see his *Autobiography*).

Neoclassicism (new classicism) is named for

its desire to imitate the art and literature of Augustan Rome. American poets of the period, like Philip Freneau and William Cullen Bryant, often imitate the classics in form as well as subject matter. Because the educated of the eighteenth century were very familiar with the classics, the many allusions to classical literature were not lost on them. Today we need a gloss next to the poems to identify these. This is another reason why we need to study classical literature: so we can understand British and American literature.

The Christian can appreciate many of the artistic ideals of neoclassicism: its emphasis on order, symmetry, decorum, balance; its use of proportion, harmony, and unity; and its purpose in teaching man to be a better citizen. The Neoclassical age elevated organization and categorization; thus, we have not only Webster's *Spelling Book* and his *An American Dictionary of the English Language*, but also a plethora of grammar books employing strong arguments for adopting "rules" for every aspect of English grammar. Because of the love of all things classical, many of the rules of Latin were drug over into English, whether they applied or not.

This was also an optimistic age characterized by an enthusiasm for all that man could discover, invent, accomplish. Much of the writing of this period is historical and political (Thomas Jefferson, Thomas Paine, and Franklin), theological (Jonathan Edwards, Timothy Dwight), and scientific (the exploration of Lewis and Clark). This appeal to the intellect encouraged scientific observation and a reliance on science as an authority.

Deism probably arose both as a reaction to Calvinism, as well as from a desire to reconcile the old religion with the new science. America's most radical deist was Thomas Paine. Though he sounds Christian when writing the *American Crisis* pamphlets, he openly attacked Christianity in his *Age of Reason*. Though many of a deistic persuasion might mention the Creator or First Cause in their writings, it would be wrong to assume the writer a Christian. At the same time, the Christian could use the artistic ideals of the neoclassical age without embracing its deistic premises. For example, the poet Phillis Wheatley (a Negro slave) is a good example of one who wrote using Neoclassical artistic ideals while expressing her Christian faith.

Of course within the broad system of beliefs of Deism there were many differences. Thomas Paine was the most extreme example. His deism was closer to atheism. Other more positive deists include George Washington, Benjamin Franklin, and Thomas Jefferson.

Neoclassicism on the Continent was more openly hostile to Christianity than it was in England and America, so Thomas Paine's antagonism to Christianity was not kindly received in this country.

Because of Neoclassicism's love of order, clarity, regularity, and imitation of traditional forms, much excellent prose was written. In England it was the age of the essay, of oratory and satire, as well as the time when men like Wesley, Newton,

Toplady, Cowper, and Dwight wrote many great hymns.[1]

---

1. Other suggested readings during this period could include some of the following (or excerpts from them): Jonathan Edwards' sermon "Sinners in the Hands of an Angry God," Poetry of Phillip Freneau, Phillis Wheatley, and Timothy Dwight, and *The Declaration of Independence.*

ROMANTICISM

If literary movements are reactions to previous eras, Romanticism could certainly be described as a reaction to rationalism. The emphasis swung from man's reason to his emotions and with it swept away many of the attitudes of Neoclassicism.

Nature, not man's intellect, was now considered the source of all knowledge. Man was thought to receive knowledge from nature via his intuition, obviously a subjective, internal standard. Consider the drift away from orthodox Christianity in our country: in the seventeenth century, God's Word was the acknowledged authority. In the next century, man's reason was elevated to this position. Now in the nineteenth century, God was thought to reveal Himself entirely through nature, each man interpreting for himself what nature was saying. No longer was nature viewed as merely a means of displaying God's glory as part of His creation; instead nature was viewed as man's moral teacher. This view can lead to pantheism, as seen in Walt Whitman's works, and it also disparages the Bible as God's Word to man, since nature has taken its place.

Formal education is also demeaned, as we can see in the example below.

Hawk-eye, the hero of Cooper's *The Last of the Mohicans*, states very clearly his views of Christianity in a conversation with the bumbling David Gamut, who is the weakest (and, not accidentally, the only Christian) character in the book. He has been disputing with David over Calvinism. David wants to know Hawk-eye's authority for his remarks. I will quote a small snippet here below.

> "Book!" repeated Hawk-eye, with singular and ill-concealed disdain. "Do you take me for a whimpering boy at the apron string of one of your old gals; and this good rifle on

my knee for the feather of a goose's wing, my ox's horn for a bottle of ink, and my leathern pouch for a cross barred handkercher to carry my dinner? Book! What have such as I, who am a warrior of the wilderness, though a man without a cross, to do with books? I never read but in one, and the words that are written there are too simple and too plain to need much schooling; though I may boast that of forty long and hard-working years."

In this conversation (and others preceding) we learn several things about Cooper's romantic viewpoint. First of all, he views nature as God's only revelation to man (therefore, his teacher). Nature alone is his "book." He views Bible reading as for sissies (like David), and he openly condemns Calvinism (the Christianity of his day) as the "belief of knaves, and the curse of an honest man." It is no surprise that the one Christian in the book is a goofy character.

Elsewhere we learn Cooper's ideas about morality: the Indians should not be condemned for scalping people in cold blood because that is the "gift" of their race.

Recognizing these elements of Cooper's philosophy should not spoil the reading for the Christian. Instead, it equips the reader. Cooper is saying something about God and about man. If the Christian thinks the story is merely about love and adventure in the woods, he has missed what Cooper was about. The book is a great example of American romanticism, and for that reason alone should be read. It is an important book (but not necessarily a great book) in our literary and historical and philosophical past. Part of the reason America is where it is today is because of the influence of Cooper and others like him. But knowing this does not have to ruin the "story." The reader can still enjoy and admire the courage of Cora, the sacrifice of Uncas, the devotion of Chingachgook, etc. When the author creates a hero who despises Christianity, he is making a very clear statement about his mission. The astute reader will keep his wits about him as he enters into the story.

Men's shifts in thinking are not limited to literature; if you look at paintings from this period, nature is predominant. A good example of American Romanticism expressed in art is Albert Bierstadt's landscape paintings of the vastness of the Rocky Mountains and Yosemite Valley. America's frontier was opening up for all to travel and see, and it was glorious.

Romanticism views man as basically good, not fallen, and his corruptions are seen as the result of the bad influences of "man-made" institutions like marriage, schools, and governments. Therefore, in the romantic worldview, man the individual is considered more significant or important than man in community. Man is seen optimistically as getting morally better and able to overcome his problems through looking in to himself. This follows, because if man is basically good, he should be able to find more and more goodness within himself. This idea supports primitivism, which is the belief that man in nature is more perfect than man in society (Rousseau's noble savage). This is why society is seen as the real problem, not the sinful heart of man.

Individualism and an emphasis on imagination are at the heart of romanticism. The hero in romantic literature is something of a rebel against tradition and society. He is often in isolation, pitted in some conflict against the establishment, and finding nobility within to rise above his circumstances. Consider Hester Prynne in *The Scarlet Letter*, Natty Bumppo in *The Last of the Mohicans*, or Thoreau at his Walden Pond. The individual and all his unique feelings are at the center. Emotion and intuition are elevated above the Neoclassical emphasis on fact and logic. The individual is no longer accountable to anything other than his own intuition, and because man is basically good, of course his intuition is good. Though we have been brought up in this country to admire individualism as a good thing, it is not good thing. Individuals are made in the image of

God, but individualism sees each man as the center of all of life. Christians are to love community, biblical authority, and godly submission. Individualism emphasizes each man for himself, doing what is right in his own eyes, and like Walt Whitman (who pushed this view of man to its unhappy conclusion), rejoicing in himself alone.

Like other periods of literature, there are great differences in beliefs among those we call the romantics. Though many had this unbiblical and unrealistic view of man, some writers like Edgar Allen Poe, Herman Melville, and Nathaniel Hawthorne had a much more pessimistic (though not necessarily more accurate) view of man, God, and the world. This cynical view of man is in sharp contrast to the prevailing optimism.

Because of the Romantic era's emphasis on breaking from tradition, many new forms of literature arose. Originality and spontaneity, an emphasis on imagination (as well as a love for ancient legends) all contributed to this notable period in American literature. Hawthorne and Poe made the American short story notable. Washington Irving's sketches caused American literature to be noticed in Europe. Cooper was read for his lavish descriptions of the frontier, making the American novel respectable abroad. And poetry flourished.

But Romanticism is man-centered. It denies the depravity of man, the deity of Christ, the inspiration of the Bible. It looks to man as the means of eradicating evil, and it sees man as having limitless possibilities. Emerson, Thoreau, and Whitman (the Transcendentalists) did much to propagate these ideas: Emerson particularly in his traveling lectures, Thoreau in his Walden experience, and Whitman in his blasphemous, free-form poetry of self-worship and unrestrained exultation of man ("the sweat of these armpits more precious than prayer") in "Song of Myself."

Though I have mentioned many blatant examples of the dangerous views of the Romantic worldview, I hasten to add that much of the literature of the day can be enjoyed with great profit and enjoyment. Many of the authors did not become antagonistic to Christianity, though they adopted the style of Romantic writing.[1]

---

1. Besides the authors mentioned above, you might want to consider some of the following: Washington Irving's *Sketchbook*, Selections of poetry of William Cullen Bryant, particularly "Thanatopsis," Selections of poetry of James Russell Lowell, Oliver Wendell Holmes, John Greenleaf Whittier, Henry Wadsworth Longfellow, Thomas Bailey Aldrich's *Story of a Bad Boy*.

AMERICAN REALISM
AND NATURALISM

Some consider the outcome of the War Between the States as the cause of the end of the romantic view of man. The South was devastated, and man did not look too good in the midst of all of the rubble, no matter what side he was on. Romanticism did not answer any of man's questions about life and sin. The war had removed all doubt about the innate goodness of man. The post-war era is considered the beginning of the period of realism.

During this period man began to question the very existence of God. This is the period of Darwin's theory of evolution receiving wide acceptance, of the development of higher criticism (man applying the scientific method to the Bible), and of religious liberalism. Because man had come to be viewed as an animal (thanks to Darwin), man was thought to be governed by instinct, not reason, and influenced heavily (if not solely) by his environment and heredity. The universe was no longer considered to be man's teacher, as it was in the romantic period, but rather as a collection of impersonal forces, hostile to man. Man was merely the result of time and chance, caught in a machine over which he had no control. And of course, this view affected the literature of the day.

The realists believed that literature should record life factually, realistically, with no shades of romance, no subjective emotional overtones. They wrote about common people in normal, everyday situations. No more great heroes, no more great adventures. Rather, life as it really is. The romantic depicted heroes with honor, dignity, beauty, and strength, but the realist tended to write with cold, clinical objectivity, just recording events with no commentary. Some writers emphasized the depressing aspects of life among the poor and in the prisons, and they used characters from among the common people who were struggling to survive.

Some works have a more pessimistic view than others, embracing Darwinism openly.

Though Mark Twain was a realist who made a great deal of fun of romantics, especially James Fenimore Cooper (be sure to read Twain's essay "The Literary Offenses of James Fenimore Cooper"), he still bemoaned the lack of romanticism in his wonderful collection of essays and sketches entitled *Life on the Mississippi*.

Bret Harte adopts an amoral tone in his story "The Outcasts of Poker Flat," where a gambler and a prostitute who have been run out of town suddenly become virtuous and give their lives to save the others who are trapped with them in the snow.

Of course the realists can be very entertaining. Some of O. Henry's short stories are very memorable; and some of them are very depressing, dealing with suicide and hopelessness. Mark Twain became more pessimistic the older he got, eventually losing all his faith in God and man. This is evident in his works.

Naturalism is what has been called "sordid realism." It is determinism and Darwinism applied to literature. While the realists sought to record life objectively as a scientist would, the Naturalists emphasized blind fate, the power of heredity and environment over man, and a pessimistic view of life as merely propagating the species.

Someone has aptly said that Jack London wrote about animals as though they were people and people as though they were animals. In his short story "The Law of Life" he describes an Indian tribe's practice of abandoning the aged for the wolves to devour. This kept the elderly from becoming a burden to the tribe. If man is just an animal, isn't it fitting that he is treated like one? "It was the law of all flesh. Nature was not kindly to the flesh. She had no concern for that concrete thing called the individual. Her interest lay in the species, the race." This is Darwinism in literature.

Also influenced by Naturalism, Stephen Crane is pessimistic about the very existence of God in his poetry.

A man said to the universe:
"Sir, I exist!"
"However," replied the universe,
"The fact has not created in me
A sense of obligation."

In another poem of Crane's, he portrays God as building the world as a ship and forgetting to add the rudder to His creation because He got distracted. As a result, the world is a cosmic joke: a rudderless ship with a "ridiculous" lack of purpose. In this poem it very easy to see not only what Crane thinks of God, but what he thinks of the world and man's significance as well. This is an important backdrop to reading *The Red Badge of Courage* where Crane depicts man's courage and cowardice as merely instincts, reactions to the environment and not springing from any knowledge of what is right or true.

Christians must engage with such unbiblical thinking in order to refute it. Of course we know that the world is fallen, and that man apart from

Christ is without hope in the world. But the Christian has hope, because God has sent a Savior into the world. The realist simply looks at the world, assuming that is all there is, and frequently despairs.[1]

---

1. Other authors and suggested readings: Bret Harte's "The Luck of Roaring Camp," Poetry of Sidney Lanier, Emily Dickinson, Edwin Arlington Robinson Short stories by Sarah Orne Jewett, Frank R. Stockton's "The Lady or the Tiger," Ambrose Bierce's short stories (or his *Devil's Dictionary*), Booth Tarkington's *Penrod*.

MODERNISM AND POST-MODERNISM

Modernism is the logical outgrowth of all that has gone before. As a post-World War I worldview, God and the Bible were considered irrelevant to man. Rather, man's reason and science were considered the arbitrary absolutes. Religious liberalism portrays God as a benevolent and impotent father of all men, creating a vague brotherhood among men of all religious beliefs, thus dubbing all religions equally true (or useless).

Modern man is viewed simply as the end product of evolution. This is obviously antithetical to the biblical view that man is created in the image of God to worship the Triune God of the Bible. Thus the modern worldview is pessimistic, embracing meaninglessness, futility, and despair. What ultimate purpose can there be for man if he is the product of random chance?

The literature of this period reflects this philosophical view: it embraces aestheticism (art for art's sake rather than as a means of glorifying God), has no rules to follow (who's to say what is wrong or right?), and claims no meaning or purpose for itself or for man. Modern literature often depicts the anti-hero (the man with no strengths or virtues to speak of) and embraces an amoral tone (making no judgments about good and evil). This means the protagonist seldom has qualities for the Christian reader to honor, and the author rarely comments on immoral behavior because modern man has no accepted authoritative standard.

This confusion of values in modern literature is at its best, muddled, and at its worst, openly hostile to God and his Word. The church is salt that has lost its savor; it no longer has a moral influence in our country. Modern man rejects claims of authority and accepts no absolute moral standards. Each man does whatever he deems to be right for him.

T.S. Eliot's poem *The Waste Land*, considered one of the most influential poetic works of the twentieth century, describes modern man in his meaninglessness and despair. Consider this excerpt from the first section, "The Burial of the Dead."

> *What are the roots that clutch, what branches grow*
> *Out of this stony rubbish? Son of man,*
> *You cannot say, or guess, for you know only*
> *A heap of broken images, where the sun beats,*
> *And the dead tree gives no shelter, the cricket no relief,*
> *And the dry stone no sound of water. Only*
> *There is shadow under this red rock,*
> *(Come in under the shadow of this red rock),*
> *And I will show you something different from either*
> *Your shadow at morning striding behind you*
> *Or your shadow at evening rising to meet you;*
> *I will show you fear in a handful of dust.*

Ernest Hemingway treats man as a noble animal in *The Old Man and The Sea*, much as he treats the shark. In speaking of the great shark, the old man says, "But, thank God, they are not as intelligent as we who kill them; although they are more noble and more able." Later he says, "Man is not much beside the great birds and beasts."

> Then he was sorry for the great fish that had nothing to eat and his determination to kill him never relaxed his sorrow for him. How many people will he feed, he thought. But are they worthy to eat him? No, of course not. There is no one worthy of eating him from the manner of his behavior and his great dignity.
> I do not understand these things, he thought. But it is good that we do not have to try to kill the sun or the moon or the stars. It is enough to live on the sea and kill our true brothers.

Another example of a modern poet at war with tradition is E.E. Cummings. His poetry is called cubist poetry because it seeks to imitate cubist, fragmented painting (like Picasso's), breaking the rules for poetry and English grammar alike.

Not all modern literature is pessimistic. But when we find optimism, it is generally coming from a secular humanistic and sentimental viewpoint, not from a sound biblical worldview. Unthinking Christians are sometimes prone to assume such writing is Christian simply because it is not openly hostile to the Bible. Consider Jesse Stuart's book *The Thread That Runs So True*. One Christian textbook includes a selection from this book as a good treatment of the purpose of education. But it is blatantly man-centered and humanistic. Man is not seen as having a sin problem that can only be dealt with by Jesus Christ. Rather, Stuart sees education as our savior. Consider this excerpt:

> Within this great profession [teaching], I thought, lay the solution of most of the cities', counties', states', and the nation's troubles. It was within the teacher's province to solve most of these things. He

could put inspiration in the hearts and brains of his pupils to do greater things upon this earth. The schoolroom was the gateway to all the problems of humanity. It was the gateway to the correcting of evils. It was the gateway to inspire the nation's succeeding generations to greater and more beautiful living with each other; to happiness, to health, to brotherhood, to everything!

Modernism has been followed by what we call Postmodernism. It is a continued working out of what has been worked into our country's bankrupt moral and religious views. We will have to wait to see how our own period in history will be interpreted as men look back at it from a fifty-year vantage point. It is difficult to evaluate it fully now. However, man has given up knowing the world or knowing himself through reason.

Because of relativism and the belief that there are no absolutes, each person suits himself. Secular humanism has become the religion of the day, and no one knows if truth really even exists. Man is in the middle of blindness and rebellion against his Creator. This is the end of the road, and for that we can be thankful. In his flight from God, American man has moved from Deism to a man-centered religion to no religion at all. Whenever things get to such a point, we can trust that God will act either in judgment or in mercy, and for that mercy we expectantly pray.

As Christians living in a Postmodern world where people don't even believe they have souls, we have a ripe opportunity to proclaim the victorious gospel of Jesus Christ. We need to pray for the church to rise up and proclaim this gospel once again. And we need to raise sons and daughters who will write, preach, teach, and sing it to their children and their grandchildren. Studying literature is one way to prepare them to do this, and we want to teach them to study literature to the glory of God, not despairing like the pagans around us, but rejoicing that God rules the world and will glorify His name in all the earth.[1]

---

1. Other suggested readings: Poetry by Carl Sandburg, Robert Frost
Willa Cather's *My Antonia*, Essays by H.L Mencken, Thornton
Wilder's *Bridge Over San Luis Rey*.

IN SUMMARY

One of the ways I tested my students in literature class was to give them a final exam in which they had to identify the worldview from an unfamiliar piece of literature. I did not disclose the author or the name of the piece, but I asked them to identify and refute the worldview. This was always a great delight to me when the students found and dismantled the false worldview. And this really is the goal: to enable them, by the grace of God, to distinguish good from evil and to be able to completely answer all the objections. Of course we want them to become great writers themselves, showing the unbelievers all the wonders of creation. But before they can do that, they must immerse themselves in all kinds of literature and learn to think about what they read. It is my hope that this little booklet will help inspire you and your students to do this.

APPENDIX

One way to illustrate the differences in literature is to use a simple diagram like the one below.

	Puritanism	Neoclassicism	Romanticism	Realism	Modern/Post-Modern
Worldview	Christian	Deism	Unitarianism	Darwinism	Secular Humanism
God	Christian	Clock-winder	Within man	Atheistic	Atheistic
Man	Fallen	Basically good	Perfectable	Animal	Animal
Nature	God's creation	Our model	Our teacher	Hostile	Materialism
Bible	God's Word	Good book	Not God's Word	Irrelevant	Irrelevant
Authority	Bible	Reason	Intuition	Reason/Science	Relativism

A FEW
HELPFUL RESOURCES

C.S. Lewis has some tremendous resources to offer, and though his subject is British literature, it teaches us to think Christianly about all kinds of literature. Some of his works that have been of particular help to me are *The Discarded Image*, *A Preface to Paradise Lost*, and *English Literature in the Sixteenth Century* (the introduction is particularly helpful).

I have used the *Oxford Companion to American Literature* and the *Oxford Companion to English Literature*. These are encyclopedias to literature, including information on authors, works, and literary terms. They often describe Christian writers as narrow and praise them back-handedly.

A good handbook to literature is a must. I have used both Holman's *A Handbook to Literature*, as well as the *Harper Handbook to Literature*. I am sure there are other good ones out there as well.

Books written from a Christian perspective that deal with specific works are truly a Godsend. These listed below can be of great help:

- Leland Ryken's book *Triumphs of the Imagination*

- Peter Leithart's books *Brightest Heaven of Invention* (on several of Shakespeare's plays), *Heroes of the City of Man* (on classical literature), and *Ascent to Love* (on Dante).

56755707R00044